anythink

D0605014

For my friend Elliot Barrett—yo ho ho!
—swashbuckler, reader, and all-around terrific guy.
—J. P.

For my two wee scallywags, Nate and Emmett,
and for everyone on deck who brought our ship home safely:
Liz, Jean, Ashley, Rich, and Allen.
—G. R.

A FEIWEL AND FRIENDS BOOK
An Imprint of Macmillan

Library of Congress Cataloging-in-Publication Data Available

ISBN: 978-1-250-00515-1

Feiwel and Friends logo designed by Filomena Tuosto

First Edition: 2013

The art was created with pencil, Sumi ink, watercolor oilstick, and pastels on paper.

10 9 8 7 6 5 4 3 2 1

mackids.com

A Pirate's Guide to Recess

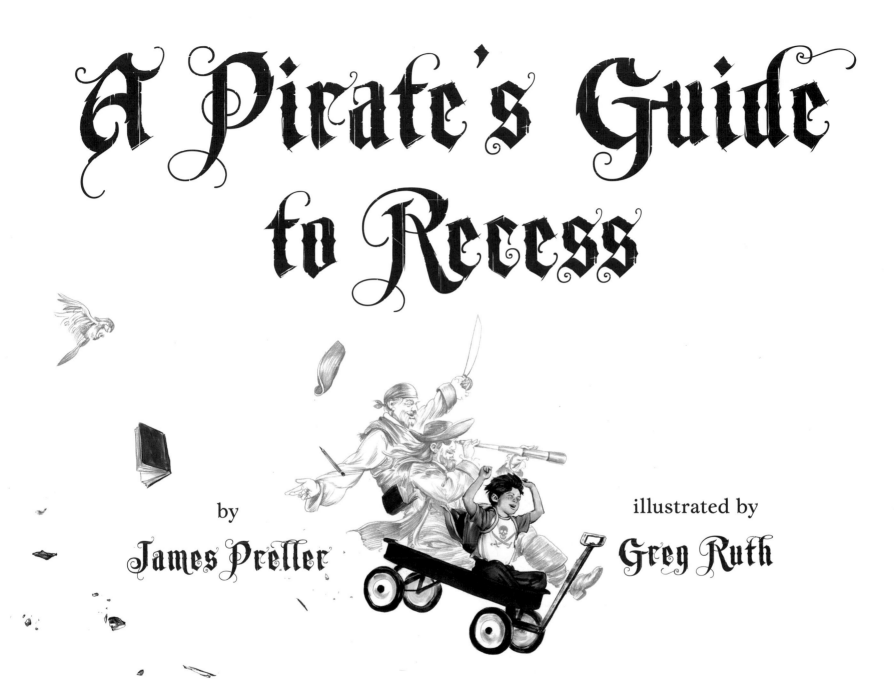

by

James Preller

illustrated by

Greg Ruth

FEIWEL AND FRIENDS

NEW YORK

"Steady now, boys,"

said Captain Red.

"It's near the merry hour."

"Sorry, Molly. Lads first.

Gangway, lubbers!"

"Double quick now, me buckos," cried Red.
"Swab the deck, swash the buckles."

"Aye, aye, Cap'n Red," the merry
crew replied.

"Weigh anchor, lads.

Hoist the Jolly Roger.

It's treasure we seek—and adventure!"

And so the crew sailed upon a wild sea.

Captain Red gave a shout.

"Ye thar, up in the crow's nest!

What say ye, lookout?"

"I fear it's Molly and her gruesome mates!"

the lookout cried.

"Bring 'em near," Red ordered.

"Let me set me deadlights on 'em!"

"Arrrr,"

Red muttered.

"Rapscallions all."

"Ahoy, there!" Red called to Molly.

"Surrender now to Cap'n Red—

the filthiest, most foul-smellin' pirate

of the seven seas!"

Molly laughed . . .

and her gang gave rude reply.

"Arrrr, then it's a
fight you'll get!"

"Silly lad,"
Molly called back.
"We only wish to play!"

Alas, Red's crew had no stomach for swordplay.

They shook in their boots most fearfully.

"Call yourselves pirates?!" Red thundered.

"Ye will fight, or walk the plank!"

To keep the peace, Red's crew turned
against their bloodthirsty captain.

"What's this? Mutiny?
I've been hornswaggled
by scallywags and brutes!"

"Don't scowl so, sweet Red!" Molly said.

"We're just having a little yo ho ho."

"Untie me now, Molly!" Red fumed.

"Promise to play nice?"

"No nay ne'er!" Red roared.

"Then marooned ye be, Red,
cast adrift on the open sea."

Brinnnnng! Brinnnnng! The bell sounded.

"**Blimey!** Hear that, Molly?

Ye can't leave me here.

I'll dry up like a raisin."

"Play again tomorrow?" Red asked.

"Aye, Red, on my mark.

We'll play tomorrow."

"**Yar!** To school, then," Red said.

"And to more adventures!" Molly cried.

Homework! A Pirate's Vocabulary

AHOY
hello

AVAST
stop

BILGE RAT
a rat living in the lowest, filthiest
part of the ship

BLIMEY
an expression of surprise

BUCKO
a friend

CROW'S NEST
a platform near the top of the mast
to give a lookout a better view

DEADLIGHTS
eyes

DOUBLE QUICK
in a hurry

GANGWAY
a warning to step aside; also,
the main walking paths along
the deck of a ship

GROG
drink

GRUB
food

HANG THE JIB
frown

HEARTIES
fellow sailors, or friends

HEAVE TO
command to bring the ship
to a halt

HORNSWAGGLE
to cheat